MY MOM

...the best mom ever!

BY LAUREN VENA

This book is dedicated to all of the amazing moms
around the world,
and the children who love them.

To My Hubby Joe.
Thank you for always being so supportive
and being my #1 Fan. I love you xo

To My Kids Chloe & Travis.
Thank you for making me a Mommy.

Thank you for Loving me unconditionally when mommy is a bit messy, crazy, silly, busy, and perfectly imperfect.

You are my everything and I love you to the moon, the stars, and back!

Published by Inspired Girl Books
821 Belmar Plaza, Unit 5 Belmar, NJ 07719
www.inspiredgirlbooks.com

Inspired Girl Books is honored to bring forth books with heart and stories that matter. We are proud to offer this book to our readers; the story, the experiences, and the words are the author's alone.

ISBN: 978-1-7350944-4-1

Iillustrations by Dilyana Aleksandrova of simplydikka
Typesetting by Roseanna White Designs

Library of Congress Control Number: 2020915018

This is my mom.
She is the best mom ever!

SNOOZE
SNOOZE
SNOOZE

She wakes up early every morning
to get us ready for school.

My mom cooks the most delicious homemade frozen waffles *from scratch*!

She's a great multitasker. While screaming at us to brush our teeth and put our shoes on, she's calling dad to say good morning, feeding the dogs, and making her coffee.

My mom is also a professional performer.
She could stand on one leg while holding
her other knee while singing in the highest pitch
sound every time she steps on a Lego brick.
We get a whole concert almost every day!

AAAAAHHH

She always makes sure
we look our best
for school.

And she always knows when we forget our lunches,
or our homework, or need one more kiss!
Mommy to the rescue!

ALEXA!!!
ALEXA?!
??
MATH

OMG! I almost forgot to tell you about my mom's best friend! Yep! Alexa!! Mom doesn't understand my homework Alexa! I get sick Alexa! She calls her for everything!!! We want another dog and daddy says NO...Alexa!!!

My mom loves us so much!
No matter what she's always up for company...

And not just when she's in the bathroom. She loves having us around her all the time. My mom loves to cuddle on the couch with the whole family watching a movie while drinking her Mama Juice. For some reason she doesn't let me take a sip, but she loves it!

My mom's heart is so big she wouldn't even hurt a spider.
In fact if dad isn't home to set it free outside,
we just shut the door and let it be.

On weekends my mom goes to work in total disguise.
She paints her face and wears fancy clothes.

My mom is a Makeup Artist. She always tells us she's "making the world beautiful." But the truth is people just let her paint on their face instead of paper.

But I love when she comes home and takes that weird paint stuff off her face. I see all the scribble lines on her forehead, the bean bags under her eyes, and those creepy caterpillars are off her lashes and she's back in daddy's pajamas...

My mom, she looks
SOOOOO BEAUTIFUL!!!!
She is just perfect in every way!!

YES!
Pizza tonight!!
MY MOM IS THE BEST!!!
PIZZA
PIZZA

The End

Lauren Vena is a renowned makeup artist, who has worked with brands including Mac, Chanel, Dior, Nars, and Clarins to name a few. She has done makeup on everyone from celebrities to brides to everyday women!

She has traveled the country as an artist and educator, and is best known for doing makeup for media, editorial, weddings, Bar and Bat Mitzvahs, and photoshoots of all kinds.

But she is proudest to say she is a wife and mother. Her debut children's book, *My Mom...the best mom ever!* was written through the eyes of her children, and as reminder to moms and kids that there is nothing better, stronger, or more special than unconditional love.

Learn more at http://LaurenVena.com.

CPSIA information can be obtained
at www.ICGtesting.com
Printed in the USA
LVIC060409201020
669243LV00008B/36